Maudie And The Green Children

First published simultaneously in Great Britain and Canada
by Tradewind Books Limited
29 Lancaster Park, Richmond, Surrey TW19 6AB, England,
and Tradewind Books Limited
2216 Stephens Street, Vancouver, British Columbia V6K 3W6, Canada

Typography by Treld Pelkey Bicknell

Set in Garamond by R&B Creative Services

Printed in Singapore by Imago Publishing

10 9 8 7 6 5 4 3 2 1

Cataloguing-in-Publication Data
for this book is available from
The British Library

Canadian Cataloguing in Publication Data

Mitchell, Adrian, 1932-
Maudie and the green children

ISBN 1-896580-06-8

I. Hamman, Sigune. II. Title
PZ7.M68Ma 1996   j823'.914   C95-11082-8

MAUDIE AND THE GREEN CHILDREN

Adrian Mitchell

Illustrated by Sigune Hamann

London and Vancouver

My name it is Maudie Hessett. My mam is a widow woman, keeps pigs. We live right here in Woolpit.

Some call me simple. That's all right. Simple folk are lucky folk if they don't get troubled. An old monk told me that and he give me a shilling. So bless me, I don't mind being called simple.

I'm full-grown now, but this story happen to me some stounds ago when I was five going on six. I know the year were 1499 because Mother Marchant say the world were going to end, but it didn't.

*H*arvest time.
It were a hot old day. The corn all gold and
sickles flashy in the sun. Red faces dripping
off with sweat. Mam sent me off with the big jug to

fetch more cider from home. I were worried. The
path to our cottage run right by the old wolf-pit.
They used to trap wolves there when there was
wolves to trap.

As I went by the wolf-pit edge, I heard a nashun noise from down there. Not wolves. It weren't a howling. More a kinda mewling, And a tingerling sound like of little bells.

I ain't frit of kittens nor bells. So down I goes, into the wolf-pit. Slid down on me bum.

They was sitting on the sand by a bunch of bracken up against the wall of that pit.

I saw the Green Children.

*T*here was a girl about ten and a boy about nine. They had on these little thin silky tunics. The girl were talking a language I never heard. It was like bells were hanging off her tongue. The boy were crying like a kitten or two.

Their legs and arms and faces were dusty green. Their eyes were a dark, deep green. Even their hair was a greeny colour.

I told 'em I was Maudie Hessett. They went all quiet and stared at me like a viper. I wanted to touch them, they were that sweet to look at. But I could see they'd be troubled by that.

So I blew 'em a kiss and clumb up out the pit and run back to the harvest. Nobody believe me at first. They laughed at me wicked. Howsumever they come in the finish and I show 'em my Green Children.

Big Alfric pick up the Green Children and put 'em in his haycart. Me and Mam got up with 'em. Alfric gee up his oxen and off we ride.

Everyone follow us, jumping up, staring and shouting all the way to Sir Richard's big house. The Green Children just hug on to each other and they don't look at anyone and they don't make no noise.

Alfric took us into Sir Richard's Great Hall. I never been there before. There was long-legged dogs and ladies and soldiers all scaly silver. Sir Richard was playing at the chess, but he leap up like a partridge when he see the Green Children. He try to talk to 'em, but all he gets is tingling bells from the girl and miaows from the boy.

Sir Richard reckon they come from a far country. So they must be hungry. So he call for food.

They was shown good pork. They push it away. They was shown eggs. They made awful faces. They was shown cheese and salty mutton and bread and honey and milk. They held their noses.

They wouldn't eat nothing till they see a platter of ordinary old green beans. Then they scoff the lot.

Sir Richard axed my mam to look
after the Green Children and she
say yes. They slept with me on
the straw.

At first they only took beans and
water. Later on they learned to eat
other human food.

The girl was quiet and quick on her
toes. She liked the flowers but she
didn't pick 'em like other folk, she just
touch 'em and smile to herself.

The boy were a bit of a watcher.
In winter all the other boys got bones
and strap them on their shoes and take
a big pointy staff and slide over the ice
fast as seagulls. But that green boy just
watched.

I think he were simple like me.
But he were clever at some things,
like hiding.

A Doctor came all the way from Dunwich to see the Children. He looked at 'em best as he could. But they wouldn't let him touch 'em.

The Doctor told my mam the boy were sickening of something. He said he would like to take the girl and show her at the Fair. He take out a little bag with golden money. But Mam and me say we'd be rot if we let the girl go. We sent that old Doctor packing.

Now the Children began to eat all kinds of food, but no meat. Bit by bit they were losing their green colour.

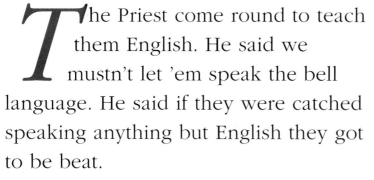

*T*he Priest come round to teach them English. He said we mustn't let 'em speak the bell language. He said if they were catched speaking anything but English they got to be beat.

The girl learn fast. The boy were slower and sometimes he got beaten mortal bad.

When they could speak English, they told me and Mam how they come to Woolpit. They say they come from somewhere called Merlin Land where there's no sun and no moon. It's always evening time and the green people do live there.

One day they were bathing in a wide river when they see a bright light on the other side of the water and they hear the sound of deep singing bells and so they follow the light and they follow the bells over the river and down a cave and into the sunshine of our wolf-pit. But the cave closed up behind them so they couldn't go home no more.

Now the Priest got riled and say there ain't no place as Merlin Land and the Children better be baptised right away now and start talking sense.

But the boy was sick and then he was very sick and then he just fade away and die. Mam said: "He were a sad boy, but he were a good boy." The Priest baptise the girl Selivia. But we call her Sal.

Well a lot later Sal turn fifteen and I turn eleven and a miller from Lynn come visiting and he marry our Sal and he take her off to Lynn. And we do miss her dancing about the place and I cry so much it take a blanket to sop it all up. Howsumever, her miller seem a good man and kind.

*B*ut two year later our Sal come back to us. The Lynn folk thought she were a witch and chased her out with stones but what do they know? And her miller man, he stay back in Lynn.

Sal show us her new baby. It were a boy with grassy green skin and dark, deep green eyes. Sal call him Ulf, after my Dad who were killed in the forest way long ago.

*U*lf grew to be five and a bonny lad. Lot of the time Sal left him with me while she went off, I never ask where to.

One day that bully Godric tease our little Ulf. He go on and on. He pinch Ulf's greeny skin and he call him Cabbage Face. So I pick up old Godric and I chuck him in the village duckpond and when he come out he were greener than a frog. I may be simple, but I'm a strong lass.

A few nights later I hear Sal get up in the night. She pick up Ulf and she take him outside. I pretend to be sleeping for a bit, then I follow them. It were a full moon and I seen 'em walking through the trees. And I knew they were heading for the Wolf-pit.

Down in the corner of the pit Sal pull back some bracken. There were a dark hole like a mouth. Sal and Ulf crawl in.

I give 'em some time, then I was down in that cave and crawling like a beetle down a dark tunnel till suddenly I find myself in a cave bigger than Sir Richard's hall and a wide green river at my feet. And the cave were shining with a soft and greeny light.

And I see Sal swimming, with Ulf hanging on to her back. And I see them climbing up the bank on the far side and I see them vanish into the green distance. But I can't swim, so I couldn't follow no further. I stood there a whiles, and then off home.

Now my Mam's died and I got a baby of my own and her name it is Maudie. I often tell her the story of the Green Children.

One day I'm going to take her down in the Wolf-pit. One day, when we've learned ourselves to swim.